For my family

-K.O.

To anyone who has to do chores

The Little Polar Bear
Copyright © 2023 by Kyle Otten

Written by Ashley, Felicity, and Kyle Otten
Illustrations copyright © 2023 by Kyle Otten
Title: Time for Chores - by Ashley, Felicity, and Kyle Otten

Summary: Everyone does chores. This book is made to try to ease young kids into making the tasks more fun.

Copywriter: Erica Douglas

Art done in graphite, Procreate, and Indesign
Text set in Domine

This book is a work of fiction. Any references to names and places are used fictitiously. Names and places are products of the authors' imagination.

Visit us online at TheLittlePolarBearShop.com

Book #1 - Time for Chores

The Little Polar Bear

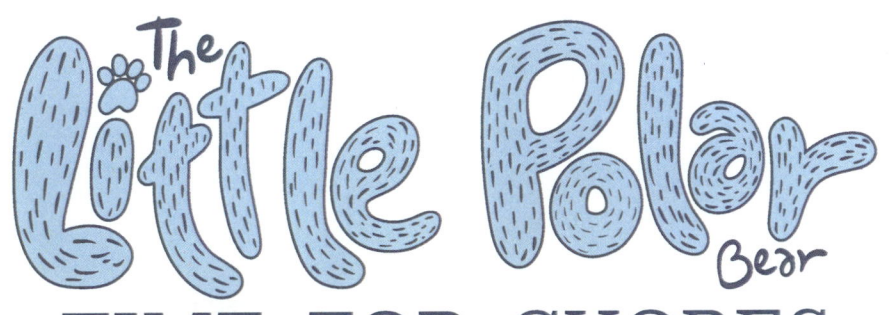

TIME FOR CHORES

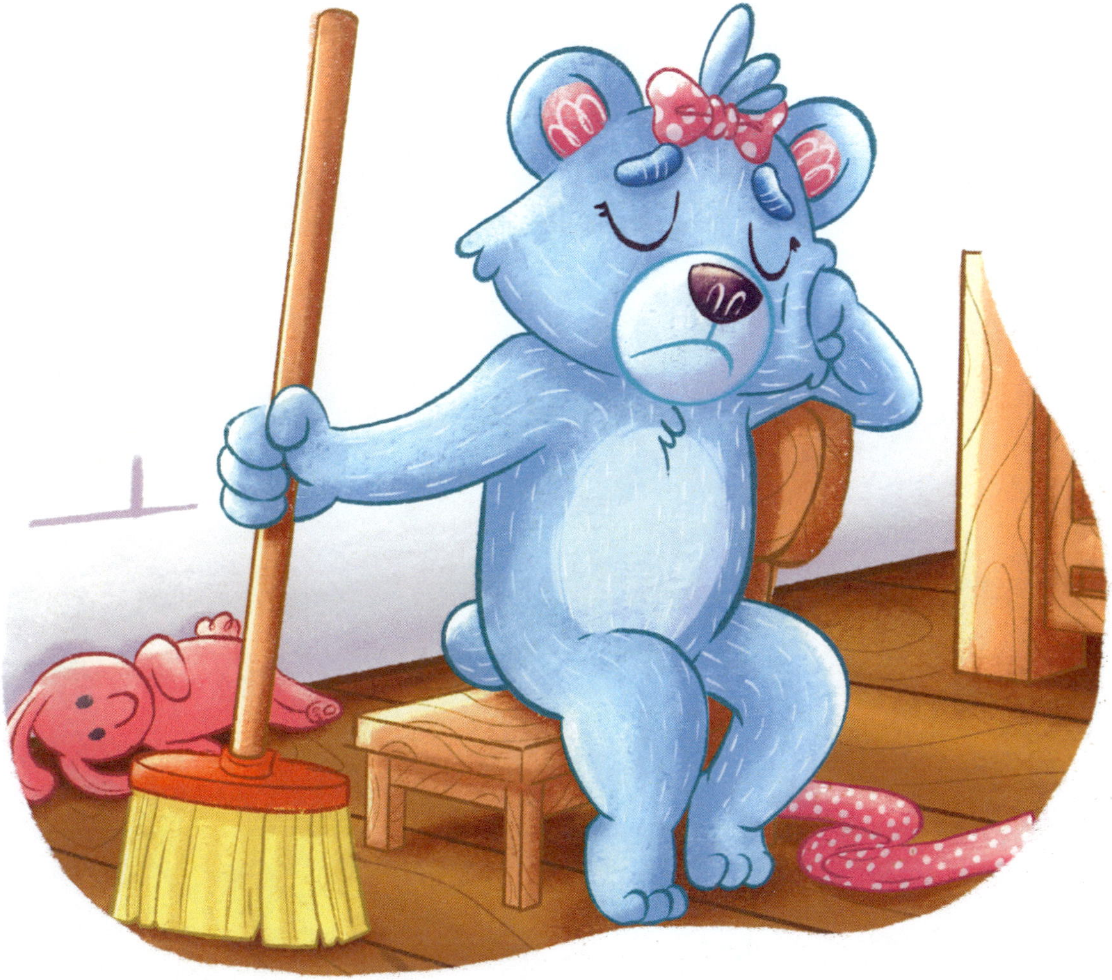

Ashley, Felicity, & Kyle Otten

In a land far away,
in the Arctic hard to find,

lived a little polar bear named Puddles, who is super kind.

Puddles is enjoying the view, just wanting to play.

Puddles's mom said, "Not until you get your chores done today."

Puddles pouted and shouted, "Please Mom, I don't like chores."

"Well, what if we start with just the floors?"

Puddles huffed and puffed, worried this will take all day.

Again, Puddles begged, "Mom, I just want to go play!"

"If we get them done, you will be free to do what you please."

Puddles replies, "Then I can go out and enjoy the breeze!"

Puddles's mom asked,
"Why don't we make a list, so none of the chores get missed?"

"Let's start with something easy to get you going.

I think we should start with all of your clothing."

Puddles thought of ways to make doing chores a game.

She grabbed the socks and matched them the same.

Puddles came up with a game to put clothes in the basket.

Puddles took out the watch that was in her mom's jacket.

She was trying to beat the timer that had just begun.

Puddles knew before time was up, the clothes would be done.

After picking up her dirty clothes in her room, she now knows it's time to pick up the broom.

"I guess I will give sweeping a chance.
The best way to do that is while I dance!"

Now that sweeping is done, Puddles can finally rejoice.
Her mom says, "Now you need to pick up all of your toys."

Her mom knows she loves
to search and find.

Puddles is doing chores,

and she doesn't even mind.

Searching for certain colors of toys is fun.

This keeps her going, till it is all done.

She's almost done, no need to rush.

It's now time to give her teeth a brush.

Her game for brushing was singing a song.

It makes the time move right along.

Puddles brushes her teeth for two minutes straight.

She thinks making her bed next would be great.

She begins by simply making her bed...

"I'm going to tuck my stuffed animals in," Puddles said.

Puddles grabs the sheets and pulls them tight.

She's so close to being done. What a delight!

Mom said, "One thing is left, my little bear.

All that's left is to brush your hair!"

Puddles was excited.
She grabbed her brush in a hurry.

"Mom, can you help me?
My hair is so furry!"

Brushing hair always makes Puddles cry.
The fur can be knotty, I won't even lie.

The question game is the best way to keep Puddles's mind clear.

Her mom thinks of a question to make the worry disappear.

Mom asks Puddles, "What color is the sky?"
She replies, "Blue," as her eyes start to dry.

After brushing her hair she said, "See that wasn't so bad, there was no reason at all for you to get sad."

Puddles was happy to go outside and play.
She has been dreaming about this moment all day!

As she walked through the meadows of grass and snow, she thought back and said, "Mom was right, that wasn't so bad, you know."

Original Concepts

Printed in the USA
CPSIA information can be obtained
at www.ICGtesting.com
LVRC091118181023
761146LV00100B/260